D0831244

BLACKBERRY FARM

HIDE & SEEK AT BLACKBERRY FARM

Jane Pilgrim

This edition first published in the United Kingdom in 1999 by
Brockhampton Press
20 Bloomsbury Street
London WC1B 3QA
An imprint of the Caxton Publishing Group Ltd.

Reprint 2000

© Text copyright MCMLII by Jane Pilgrim
© Illustrations copyright MCMLII by Hodder & Stoughton Ltd

Designed and Produced for Brockhampton Press by
Open Door Limited
80 High Street, Colsterworth, Lincolnshire, NG33 5JA

Illustrator: F. Stocks May
Colour separation: GA Graphics Stamford

All rights reserved. No part of this publication may be reproduced
or transmitted in any form or by any means, electronic or
mechanical, including photocopying, recording or any information
storage and retrieval system, without prior permission in writing
from the copyright owner.

Title: BLACKBERRY FARM, Hide & Seek at Blackberry Farm
ISBN: 1-84186-013-1

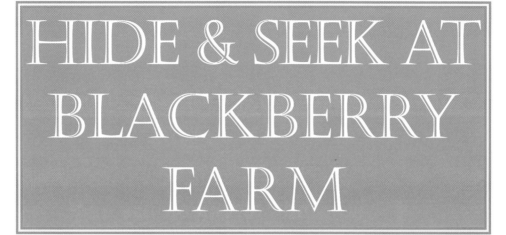

HIDE & SEEK AT BLACKBERRY FARM

Jane Pilgrim

Illustrated by F. Stocks May

BROCKHAMPTON PRESS

Lucy and Marcus Mouse had
two very fine children
called Len and Sid, and they all
lived very happily down a hole in
the corner of the big barn at
Blackberry Farm.

But one day Lucy Mouse was very alarmed to see George the kitten playing in the barn. "Go away George," she cried. "You will frighten my babies. Go away and play somewhere else." And she shook her broom at him.

Now Lucy Mouse was pretending that she was very brave, for she was really very frightened of cats. "He is a nice cat as cats go," she said to Marcus, "but one day he might forget and be a little rough with my babies." And Marcus Mouse agreed.

Len and Sid were good little
mice. But they did think it was
more fun to play all over the barn
and not just in their own little
corner. So when their mother was
busy they scampered off to play in
the straw right on the other side
of the barn.

They ran up to the top of the pile
of straw and peeped over the
edge. There asleep in the sunshine
was George the kitten.

He looked very gentle and very
soft, and not at all bad. Len and
Sid slid carefully down until they
were so close that they could
almost touch him.

The straw creaked. George's
whiskers twitched. Len and Sid
jumped back and looked again.
George opened one eye, and then
he opened the other eye. He saw
the two little mice. "Boo!" he said.
"I'm coming to play with you."

But Len and Sid thought it was
time to go home, so they
scampered up to the top of the
straw and down the other side and
across the barn and hid in an old
wheelbarrow.

And George went up over the
straw and down the other side and
across the barn, but when he came
to the old wheelbarrow, he could
not see Len and Sid anywhere.
"Miaow!" he called, "Come and
play with me!" But Len and Sid
kept very still inside the old
wheelbarrow.

When they thought that George would not notice, they nipped out of the barrow to hide behind a large bucket full of water.

But George had seen their tails flash and as they ran he jumped high in the air after them. "Now I will catch them, "he thought, and he called out: "Look out, Len and Sid, I'm coming to catch you!"

But it was a longer jump than George had thought. Poor George! Instead of landing on top of the little mice, he landed splash in the bucket of water!

And Len and Sid sat back and laughed until their whiskers ached. Then they ran home to tea and told Lucy and Marcus Mouse all about the chase. And Lucy and Marcus scolded them and told them that they were very lucky not to have been caught by George, and that they must never go over to the other side of the barn again.

SEEK AT BLACKBERRY FARM

And poor wet George had to dry
himself in front of the kitchen
fire, and no one could understand
how he had managed to get so
wet, because it was a very
sunshiny day at Blackberry Farm.
And George thought it was better
not to tell anyone what had
happened. So he didn't!